# Savitri

## A TALE OF ANCIENT INDIA

AARON SHEPARD

Illustrated by VERA ROSENBERRY

Albert Whitman & Company • Morton Grove, Illinois

In memory of Will Perry. A.S.
For Venki. V.R.

Text © 1992 by Aaron Shepard.
Illustration © 1992 by Vera Rosenberry.
Published in 1992 by Albert Whitman & Company,
6340 Oakton Street, Morton Grove, Illinois 60053-2723.
Published simultaneously in Canada
by General Publishing, Limited, Toronto.
All rights reserved. Printed in the U.S.A.
10 9 8 7 6 5 4 3 2 1

Library of Congress Cataloging-in-Publication Data
Shepard, Aaron.
Savitri: a tale of ancient India / retold by
Aaron Shepard; illustrated by Vera Rosenberry.
p. cm.
Summary: In this tale from the "Mahabharata,"
India's national epic, Princess Savitri outwits
the god of death to save her husband.
ISBN 0-8075-7251-9
1. Sāvitrī (Hindu mythology)—Juvenile
literature. 2. Mahābhārata—Biography—
Juvenile literature. [1. Sāvitrī (Hindu
mythology) 2. Mythology, Hindu.
3. Mahābhārata.] I. Rosenberry, Vera, ill.
II. Title.
BL1138.4.S28S44   1992          91-16591
294.5'923—dc20                  CIP
[398.2]                         AC

The story of the princess Savitri is one of the best-known and best-loved tales of India. It appears within *The Mahabharata,* India's great national epic, which is much like an Old Testament to the Hindus.

This epic, written down at around the time of Christ, had already been passed on orally for centuries. It arises from a time when legends were born—an age of walled cities, of sun and fire worship, and of women far more independent than later Indian culture allowed.

In India, in the time of legend, there lived a king with many wives but not one child. Morning and evening for eighteen years, he faced the fire on the sacred altar and prayed for the gift of children.

Finally, a shining goddess rose from the flames.

"I am Savitri, child of the Sun. By your prayers, you have won a daughter."

Within a year, a daughter came to the king and his favorite wife. He named her Savitri, after the goddess.

Beauty and intelligence were the princess Savitri's, and eyes that shone like the sun. So splendid was she, people thought she herself was a goddess. Yet, when the time came for her to marry, no man asked for her.

Her father told her, "Weak men turn away from radiance like yours. Go out and find a man worthy of you. Then I will arrange the marriage."

In the company of servants and councilors, Savitri traveled from place to place. After many days, she came upon a hermitage by a river crossing. Here lived many who had left the towns and cities for a life of prayer and study.

Savitri entered the hall of worship and bowed to the eldest teacher.
As they spoke, a young man with shining eyes came into the hall.
He guided another man, old and blind.

"Who is that young man?" asked Savitri softly.

"That is Prince Satyavan," said the teacher, with a smile. "He
guides his father, a king whose realm was conquered. It is well that
Satyavan's name means 'Son of Truth,' for no man is richer in virtue."

When Savitri returned home, she found her father sitting with the holy seer named Narada.

"Daughter," said the king, "have you found a man you wish to marry?"

"Yes, Father," said Savitri. "His name is Satyavan."

Narada gasped. "Not Satyavan! Princess, no man could be more worthy, but you must not marry him! I know the future. Satyavan will die, one year from today."

The king said, "Do you hear, Daughter? Choose a different husband!"

Savitri trembled but said, "I have chosen Satyavan, and I will not choose another. However long or short his life, I wish to share it."

Soon the king rode with Savitri to arrange the marriage.

Satyavan was overjoyed to be offered such a bride. But his father, the blind king, asked Savitri, "Can you bear the hard life of the hermitage? Will you wear our simple robe and our coat of matted bark? Will you eat only fruit and plants of the wild?"

Savitri said, "I care nothing about comfort or hardship. In palace or in hermitage, I am content."

That very day, Savitri and Satyavan walked hand in hand around
the sacred fire in the hall of worship.

In front of all the priests and hermits, they became husband and wife.

For a year, they lived happily. But Savitri could never forget that Satyavan's death drew closer. Finally, only three days remained. Savitri entered the hall of worship and faced the sacred fire. There she prayed for three days and nights, not eating or sleeping.

"My love," said Satyavan, "prayer and fasting are good. But why be this hard on yourself?"

Savitri gave no answer.

The sun was just rising when Savitri at last left the hall. She saw Satyavan heading for the forest, an ax on his shoulder.

Savitri rushed to his side. "I will come with you."

"Stay here, my love," said Satyavan. "You should eat and rest."

But Savitri said, "My heart is set on going."

Hand in hand, Savitri and Satyavan walked over wooded hills. They smelled the blossoms on flowering trees and paused beside clear streams. The cries of peacocks echoed through the woods.

While Savitri rested, Satyavan chopped firewood from a fallen tree. Suddenly, he dropped his ax.

"My head aches," he said.

Savitri rushed to him. She laid him down in the shade of a tree, his head on her lap.

"My body is burning!" said Satyavan. "What is wrong with me?"

Satyavan's eyes closed. His breathing slowed.

Savitri looked up. Coming through the woods to meet them was
a princely man. He shone, though his skin was darker than the darkest
night. His eyes and his robe were the red of blood.

Trembling, Savitri asked, "Who are you?"

A deep, gentle voice replied. "Princess, you see me only by the
power of your prayer and fasting. I am Yama, god of death. Now is the
time I must take the spirit of Satyavan."

Yama took a small noose and passed it through Satyavan's breast, as if through air. He drew out a tiny likeness of Satyavan, no bigger than a thumb.

Satyavan's breathing stopped.

Yama placed the likeness inside his robe. "Happiness awaits your husband in my kingdom. Satyavan is a man of great virtue."

Then Yama turned and headed south, back to his domain.

Savitri rose and started after him.

Yama strode smoothly and swiftly through the woods, while Savitri struggled to keep up. At last, he stopped to face her.

"Savitri! You cannot follow to the land of the dead!"

"Lord Yama," said Savitri, "I know your duty is to take my husband. But my duty as his wife is to stay beside him."

"Princess, that duty is at an end," said Yama. "Still, I admire your loyalty. I will grant you a favor—anything but the life of your husband."

Savitri said, "Please restore my father-in-law's kingdom and his sight."

"His sight and his kingdom shall be restored."

Yama again headed south. Savitri followed.

Along a riverbank, thorns and tall sharp grass let Yama pass untouched. But they tore at Savitri's clothes and skin.

"Savitri! You have come far enough!"

"Lord Yama, I know my husband will find happiness in your kingdom. But you carry away the happiness that is mine!"

"Princess, even love must bend to fate," said Yama. "Still, I admire your devotion. I will grant you another favor—anything but the life of your husband."

Savitri said, "Grant many more children to my father."

"Your father shall have many more children."

Yama once more turned south. Again, Savitri followed.

Up a steep hill Yama glided, while Savitri clambered after him. At the top, he halted.

"Savitri! I forbid you to come farther!"

"Lord Yama, you are respected and revered by all. Yet, no matter what may come, I will remain by Satyavan!"

"Princess, I tell you for the last time, you will not!" said Yama. "Still, I can only admire your courage and your firmness. I will grant you one last favor—anything but the life of your husband."

"Then grant many children to *me*," said Savitri. "And let them be children of Satyavan!"

Yama's eyes grew wide as he stared at Savitri. "You did not ask for your husband's life, yet I cannot grant your wish without releasing him. Princess, your wit is as strong as your will."

Yama took out the spirit of Satyavan and removed the noose.
The spirit flew north, quickly vanishing from sight.
"Return, Savitri. You have won your husband's life."

The sun was just setting when Savitri again laid Satyavan's head in her lap.

His chest rose and fell. His eyes opened.

"Is the day already gone? I have slept long," he said. "But what is wrong, my love? You smile and cry at the same time!"

"My love," said Savitri, "let us return home."

Yama was true to all he had promised. Savitri's father became father
to many more. Satyavan's father regained both sight and kingdom.
    In time, Satyavan became king, and Savitri his queen. They lived
long and happily, blessed with many children. So they had no fear
or tears when Yama came again to carry them to his kingdom.

The text typeface is Bernhard Modern.
The illustrations are ink and watercolor.
Designer: Karen Johnson Campbell.

The endsheet design is based on patterns formed
with rice flour for traditional festivals in India.